Trouble for Tuffy

A KATIE AND TED STORY

Ann Bermingham

Illustrated by Marie Burlington

THE O'BRIEN PRESS
DUBLIN

First published 1999 by The O'Brien Press Ltd,
20 Victoria Road, Dublin 6, Ireland.
Tel: +353 1 4923333; Fax: +353 1 4922777
E-mail: books@obrien.ie
Website: www.obrien.ie
Reprinted 2000, 2003.

ISBN: 0-86278-554-5

British Library Cataloguing-in-Publication Data
Bermingham, Ann
Trouble for Tuffy : a Katie and Ted story. - (O'Brien flyers ;2)
1.Children's stories
I.Title
823.9'14[J]

3   4   5   6   7   8   9   10
03   04   05   06   07   08   09

Typesetting, editing, layout, design: The O'Brien Press Ltd
Cover and internal illustrations: Marie Burlington
Printing: Cox & Wyman Ltd

CHAPTER 1

Always Trouble

Once there were twins: Katie and Ted.

Katie and Ted lived with their Mum, Dad, Baby Clare and **Tuffy**, the dog.

One day, Mum went into town. Dad was in charge. This was very bad news for Tuffy, the dog. You see, Tuffy has a job. He tries to keep Katie and Ted out of trouble. And that's not easy.

When Dad is boss, it's even
harder. Dad does not call
out, 'What are you two up to
now?' He is happy to sit with the
newspaper. If there is trouble,
Dad will sit it out. And with Katie
and Ted, there is always trouble.
Always.

'What'll we do?' asked Ted.

Now *that* is a question Tuffy hates.

'We'll do something

f-a-n-t-a-s-t-i-c,' said Katie.

'I love it when only Dad is here,' said Ted.

'Woof!' said Tuffy.

That woof means 'No!' Oh, no!

Tuffy is a very clever dog. He can think. And he can talk – in woofs.

One woof = No!

Two woofs = Yes!

Three woofs = Come and see!

Four woofs = Yippee!

Sadly, Katie and Ted do not understand a woof he says. If they did, Tuffy could keep them out of trouble. He would have a king's life. Instead, Tuffy has a dog's life.

'I've got an idea what to do,'
said Katie (Katie has lots of ideas).
'Let's have a **fight**!'

'No,' said Ted.

'You can be the winner,' said
Katie.

Ted shook his head. He knew
Katie would never let him win.

'What about chasing?'

'No.'

'House?'

'No.'

'Football?'

'No.'

'Barbies?'

'Never.'

With Katie and Ted, this could go on forever!

Then Katie said,
'I know, let's **dress up**!'

'Great idea,'
said Ted. 'Mad!'

'Woof!' said Tuffy.

Tuffy did not think it was a
great idea...

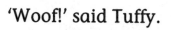

Woof!

CHAPTER 2

Dressing Up

Katie and Ted went into the spare
room. They call it the **magic** room. In
this magic room is a huge red box full
of dressing-up clothes. You can be
anyone you want in this room.

First, Ted put on a cowboy hat.
'Yee-ha! Gee up, horsey!
Yee-ha!'

Katie put on a witch's hat.

'Time for...boy soup!' she cackled.

'I want to be a **princess** now,' said Katie.

She put on her princess dress and her crown. She glided around the room with her nose in the air and a sweet smile on her face.

Ted said, 'I want to be **Count Dracula** now.'

He put on his Dracula cape and put in his Dracula teeth.  He swished and swirled and flapped his cape. He showed his teeth. He was so spooky, he scared himself.

Tuffy got sleepy and catnapped. He dreamed that he was King Tuffy, who lived with two **perfect** children in a palace made of **big** juicy bones.

Y-u-m-m-y.

Tuffy did not want to wake up – but he did. And he could not believe his dog ears! Katie and Ted were planning to go into Mum and Dad's room. They were planning to get a **necklace** so that Katie could be a real princess.

'Woof!' said Tuffy. P-l-e-a-s-e, no. Not a necklace. Not in Mum and Dad's room.

Remember the last time you went in there? Remember! Now it's a **no-go area**. And no means no. **N.O. No.**

Woof!

Oh, there's going to be trouble, big trouble. (Tuffy can always tell.)

'Woof!'

Do you think Katie and Ted listened?

Tuffy can answer that.

'Woof!'

CHAPTER 3

A Real Princess

Katie and Ted sneaked into Mum and Dad's room. Tuffy tried his best to stop them.

'Woof!' he yelped.

Katie and Ted did not notice. They were too busy looking for a necklace.

Katie knocked over Dad's talc. Ted spilt Mum's perfume.

Woof!

Then Ted said, 'Look up there, Katie! On the top shelf.'

Katie and Ted looked at the **golden box** on the top shelf.

'Let's get it!' said Katie.

'Cool,' said Ted.

'Woof!' said Tuffy. But there was no stopping them now.

Woof!

26

Yes!

Katie stood on the bed
but she could not reach the box.

Ted stood on a chair but he
could not reach the box.

Then Katie had another
one of her brainwaves. She
put the chair on the bed.
Ted held it steady
while Katie climbed
up. And with one big
swoop, she grabbed
the golden box.

Katie opened the box. There was Mum's **best** necklace. Sparkling.

'I'll just put it on for a minute,' said Katie.

'Woof!' said Tuffy. Not even for a second. This is Mum's best necklace!

Woof!

'Dracula will put it on for you,' said Ted in his best scary Dracula voice. (Ted was always trying to scare Katie but he never could.)

'Away, Dracula. I can do it. Away.'

Then to Tuffy's horror, Katie put on
Mum's best necklace. Mum's very best
necklace!

'Now I'm a real princess,'
said Katie.

'And I'm in real **trouble**,' thought
Tuffy.

CHAPTER 4

The Missing Necklace

Ted flashed his Dracula teeth.
Katie flashed Mum's best
necklace. They were the best
of twins.

Then Ted shouted, 'Dracula is after you!'

Ted chased Katie all around Mum and Dad's room. He chased her into Baby Clare's room. He chased her around every room in the house, but not the sitting room. Dad and Baby Clare were in there.

But Katie was too fast for Ted –
and Tuffy.

Katie ran into the garden. Ted
followed her. Tuffy followed him,
panting.

'Aaaha! I see you, Princess Katie. Dracula sees you behind the plum tree,' said Ted. 'I'll give you ten to get away.'

One, two, three, four, five, six, seven, eight, nine, ten.

Katie sprinted. This time she hid in Tuffy's little house at the end of the garden.

'Come out, Princess!' called Ted. 'I'll count to thirty.'

Ten, twenty, thirty.

Katie scrambled out.

'Ten, twenty, thirty,' called Ted.

'That's not **fair**,' said Katie.

'Dracula is never fair,' said Ted.
'Ha ha ha!'

Katie ran around the swings.
She jumped over the sandpit. She
jumped over the roses.

'Woooooo!' said Ted. 'Dracula is
behind you. Look!'

Katie looked. Ted ran. Ted jumped.

'Got you,' he said. 'Got you.'

THEN A TERRIBLE THING
HAPPENED. MUM'S BEST
NECKLACE WAS **MISSING**.
MUM'S VERY BEST NECKLACE.

'**It's lost!**' wailed Katie. 'It
was around my neck. Now it's
gone.'

'It can't be,' cried Ted.

'Woof, woof,' said Tuffy. It can
be. It is. Lost.

Woof, woof

'It must have fallen off when I was running,' said Katie.

'It could be **anywhere**,' said Ted, 'and Mum will be home soon.'

'Woof, woof,' said Tuffy. Yes, very soon.

Katie looked at Ted and Tuffy. Then she remembered that she was a princess. 'We must be brave. We will find the necklace. We will.'

So they looked and they
looked. They looked in Mum and
Dad's room. They looked in Baby
Clare's room.

They looked in every room in
the house, but not the sitting
room. Dad and Baby Clare were
in there.

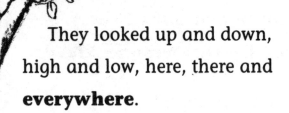

They looked up and down,
high and low, here, there and
everywhere.

'We're dead,' said
Ted. 'Mum'll be back
any minute and we've
lost her **very best necklace**.'

CHAPTER 5

Woof, Woof, Woof!

Then Tuffy sniffed something. Sniff.
He sniffed again. Sniff, sniff. It was
Mum's smell.

Tuffy panicked. What would
happen if Mum came back now? He
looked up. He looked around. He
listened.

He looked again. No Mum. Phew!
That was close!

Tuffy went back to his sniffing.

He followed his nose. Sniff.
He knew that smell. Sniff, sniff.
It was the smell of the missing
necklace! Sniff, sniff, sniff. Tuffy
was near. Tuffy was so near, he
was hot. He was a little **hot dog**!

He came to his own **little house**.
Sniff, sniff, sniff, sniff. He put his head
inside. He could not believe his eyes.
There it was! Mum's very best
necklace! Tuffy stared at it. How it
shone! He gazed at it. How it glowed!

'Woof, woof, woof!' Tuffy barked loudly. 'Woof, woof, woof!'

He wanted Katie and Ted to **come and see**.

'Woof, woof, woof!' Tuffy barked his head off.

It was useless. Katie and Ted did not know what he was woofing.

'Woof, woof, woof!'

'Shush, Tuffy,' said Ted.

'Woof, woof, woof!'

'Q-U-I-E-T. Even Dad will hear you.'

'Woof, woof, woof!' Tuffy went on trying. If only he could get Katie and Ted over to his little house.

How could he show the necklace to Katie and Ted?

First, Tuffy tried to put the necklace in his **mouth,** but he was afraid he would scratch it.

Then, he tried to push it along with his **nose,** but he was afraid it would get dirty.

The problem was this: Tuffy knew **what** he had to do. He just didn't know **how** to do it.

Tuffy looked at the necklace.
He looked at Katie and Ted. They
looked so **sad**. Tuffy did not want
them to be sad. He loved them.
He wanted them to be happy. He
wanted them to know that the
necklace was **safe**.

Time was running out **fast**. Mum would be home any minute.

Tuffy tried again. He went over to Katie. He pulled at her princess shoe. He pulled and pulled.

'I'll play later,' said Katie. 'Now we have to find Mum's necklace...'

Tuffy went over to
Ted. He pulled at his
Dracula cape. He pulled
and pulled.

'I'll play later,' said Ted.
'Now we have to find Mum's
necklace...'

Tuffy walked slowly back to his little house. He put his head down and howled. If only Katie and Ted understood! If only he could take the necklace to them!

Tuffy howled louder. He howled and howled, his howliest howl.

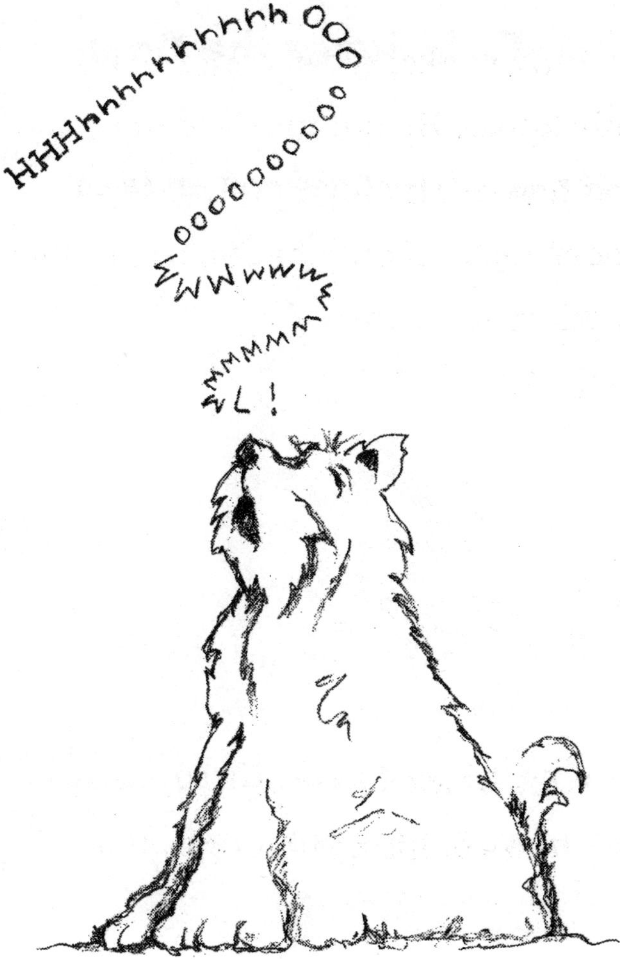
HHHhhhhhhhhhhOOOooooooooooooWWWwwwwwwwwwwwwL!

CHAPTER 6

Tuffy Saves the Day!

Then he stopped. He had an **idea**.

It was a clever idea. Tuffy is a clever dog. He would put the necklace around his own neck. He could carry it that way. He could take it to Katie and Ted. **Brilliant!**

So that is what Tuffy did.

Then he went over to Katie
and Ted with the necklace around
his neck.

Ted was in a flap and even Katie was worried.

Then they both saw it. Mum's necklace! Mum's very best necklace! There it was, gleaming in the sunlight around Tuffy's **neck**!

'Tuffy!' they both cried, 'Tuffy, you're a genius.'

Katie and Ted were so happy that they hugged Tuffy until he barked.

'Woof, woof, woof, woof!'

Yippee!

It was at times like this that Tuffy loved his job.

'Woof, woof, woof, woof!'

'Show me where you found it,
Tuffy,' Katie said.

'Woof, woof, woof,' said Tuffy.

This time Katie and Ted **did** come
and see.

'It must have fallen off when I was hiding,' said Katie.

'We never looked in Tuffy's house,' said Ted.

'Lucky for us, Tuffy did,' said Katie.

Now Katie and Ted had to tidy up fast.

'Remember – **MUM**!' cried Ted.

'Woof, woof,' said Tuffy. Run, hurry.

So with great speed, Katie and Ted sorted out Mum and Dad's room. They put the necklace back into its golden box.

They wiped up the talc and the perfume. It was as if they had **never** been in there.

Next, Katie, Ted and Tuffy went back into the magic room. They put away their dressing-up clothes.

'Woof, woof, woof, woof!' said Tuffy. **Yippee!**

Then they all went downstairs
to Dad and Baby Clare. They sat
beside them on the couch.

Katie, Ted and Tuffy were
tired, very very tired. Soon they
all fell **fast asleep**.

When Mum came home, she saw them all asleep: Katie, Ted, Dad, Baby Clare – and Tuffy.

Mum smiled.

'They must have had a nice **quiet** time...' she thought.

Tuffy has one woof to say about that.